April Puddle Stomp!

SCIENCE FAIR
RUNNER UP

Science project:
May Flowers

June Family BBQ

For Charlotte, who always draws with me.
—E.P.

A Joulia Copernicus Book

Text and illustrations copyright © 2020 by Ellie Peterson

For information about permission to reproduce selections
from this book, please contact permissions@bmkbooks.com

Boyds Mills Press
An Imprint of Boyds Mills & Kane
boydsmillspress.com

Printed in China

ISBN: 978-1-63592-136-6

Library of Congress Control Number: 2019940258

First edition

10 9 8 7 6 5 4 3 2 1

Design by Elynn Cohen

THE REASON FOR THE SEASONS

WRITTEN AND ILLUSTRATED BY Ellie Peterson

BOYDS MILLS PRESS

I'll bet you know all about them . . .

THE SEASONS . . .

You might even have a favorite!

How many there are, what they're called, when they occur . . .

But do you know what *causes* the seasons in the first place?

Perhaps you think it's that the earth is closer to the sun in summer and farther from the sun in winter.

The sun is much larger than shown here, and much farther away from Earth. If the earth was this size, the sun would be the size of a bus and it would be eight football fields away. Unfortunately, we can't show you the actual size of the sun because this book is not THAT big.

The North and South Poles experience seasons as well, but they still stay pretty cold because the sun's rays are too indirect to make them much warmer.

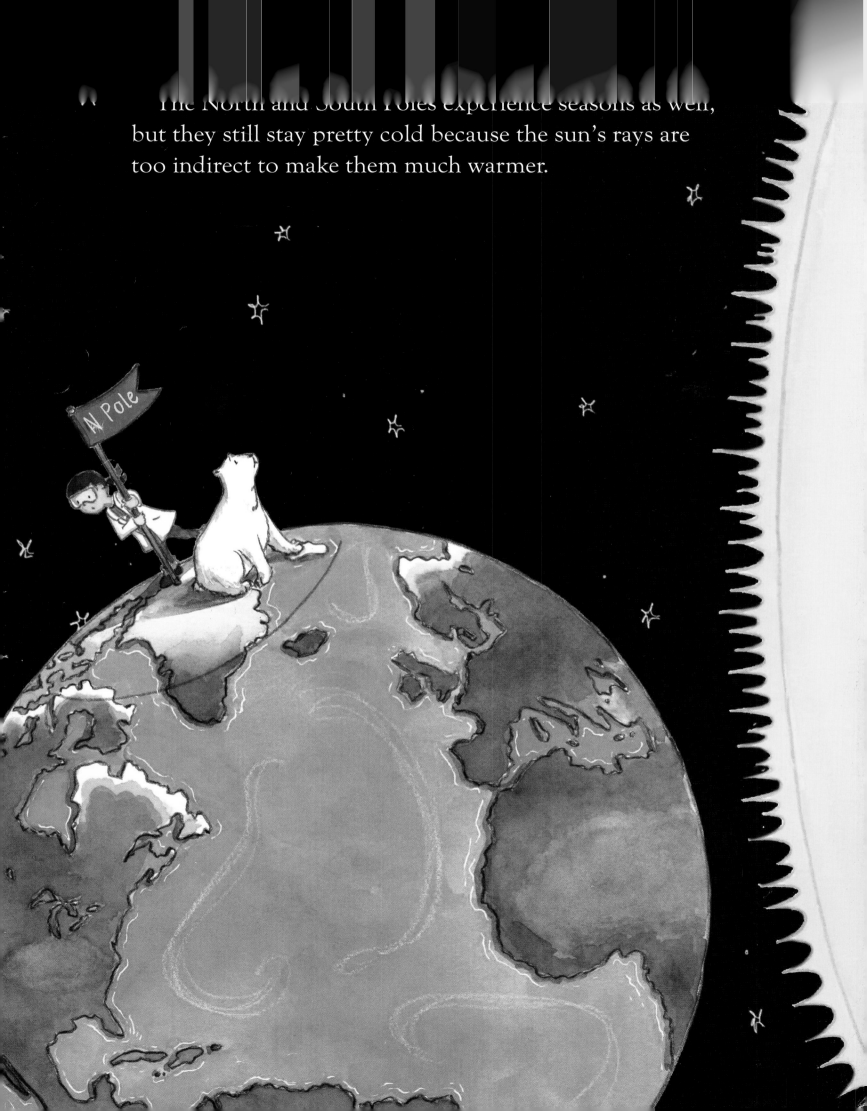

In another region, closer to the equator, the light from the sun is very direct and there is little change in the amount of light energy all year long. This area is called the Tropics, and these countries don't experience big changes in temperature from season to season, like the rest of the world.

Scientists drew two imaginary lines around the earth to show where the Tropics are located. The line south of the equator is the Tropic of Capricorn. The line north of the equator is the Tropic of Cancer.

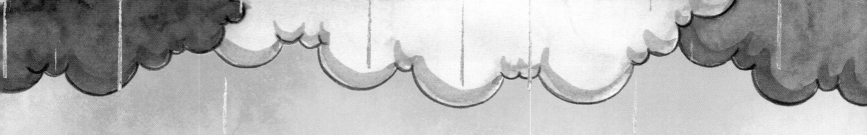

Throughout our whole history, people have relied on the seasons to mark time and the passing of each year. However, the way they define them is based on where they live and can vary greatly. Many islands and coastal areas have extra seasons like pre-spring and high summer.

Areas around the equator have a RAINY season . . .

After all, you're usually warmer when
you're closer to a source of heat.

If we had summer because Earth was closer to the sun during those months, then our whole planet would have summer at the same time. BUT IT DOESN'T! When it's cold and snowy in the Northern Hemisphere, it's downright balmy in the Southern Hemisphere. They have *opposite* seasons!

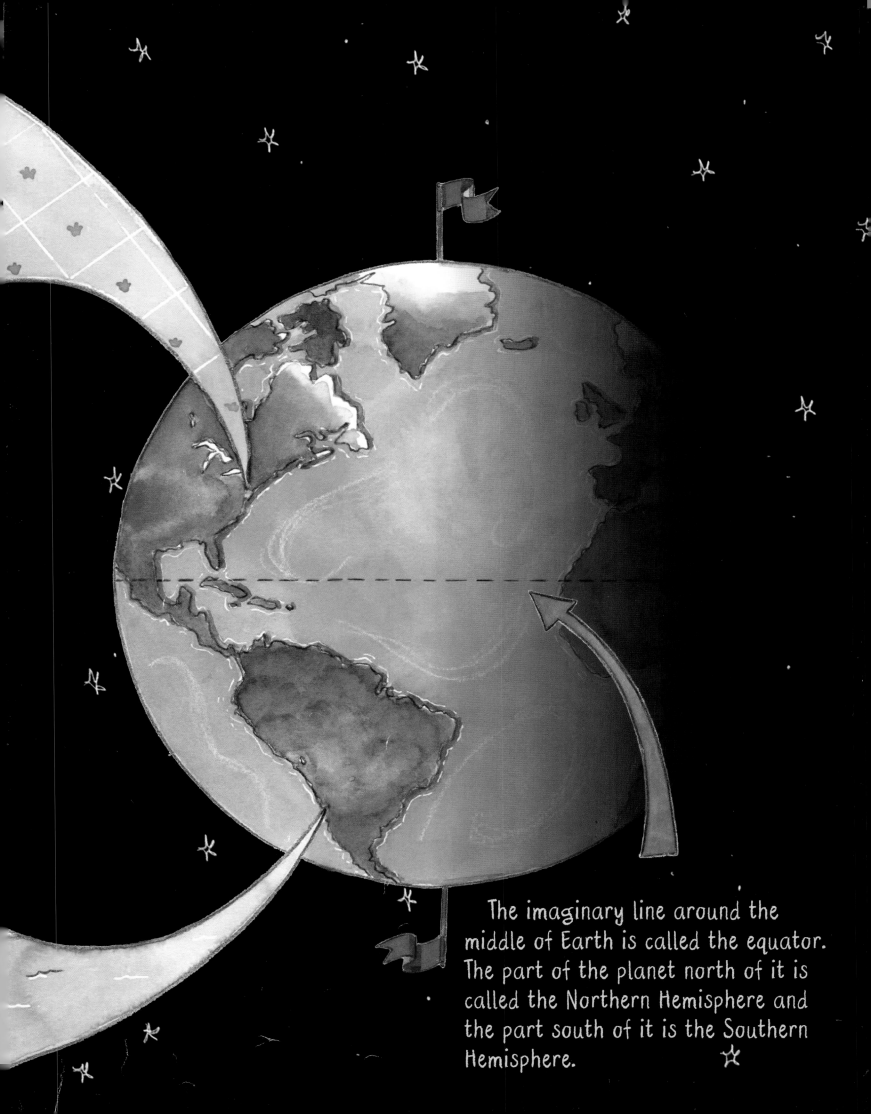

The imaginary line around the middle of Earth is called the equator. The part of the planet north of it is called the Northern Hemisphere and the part south of it is the Southern Hemisphere.

In fact, the earth is slightly *closer* to the sun in January and slightly *farther* from the sun in July.

That means that in the Northern Hemisphere, Earth is closest to the sun in winter. Seems strange, but it's true!

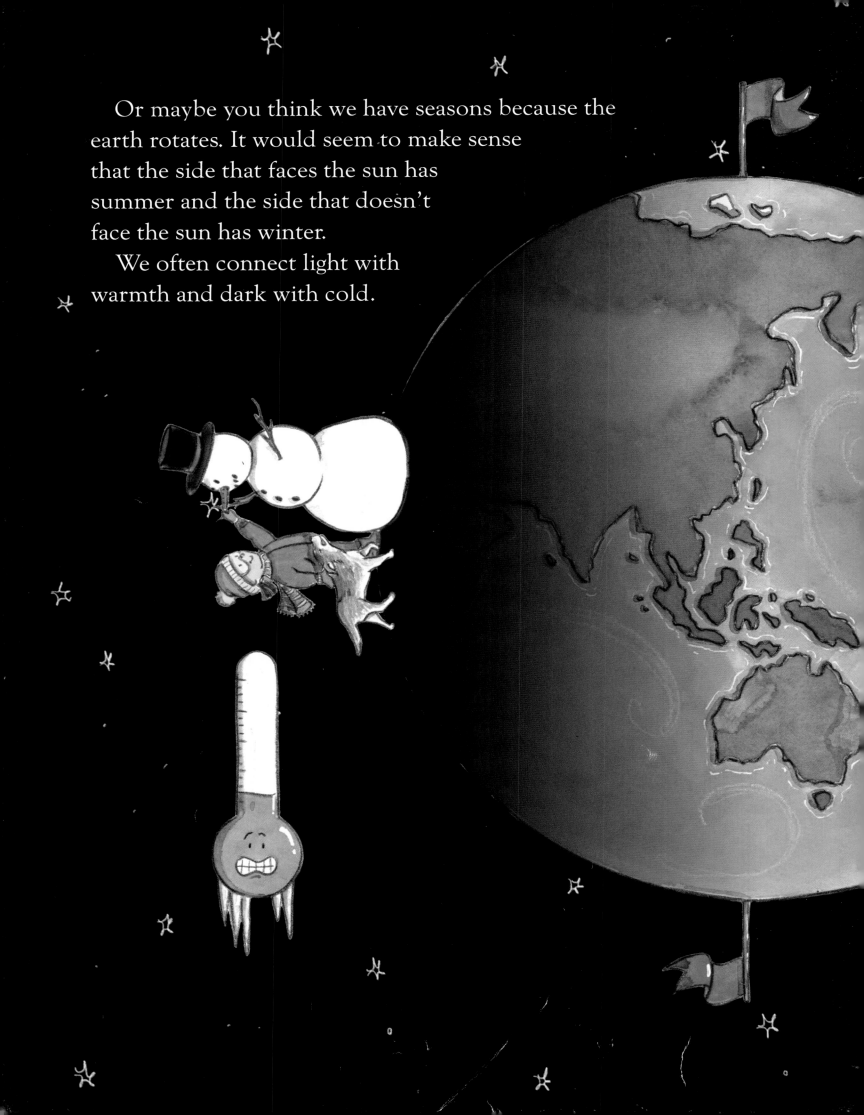

Or maybe you think we have seasons because the earth rotates. It would seem to make sense that the side that faces the sun has summer and the side that doesn't face the sun has winter.

We often connect light with warmth and dark with cold.

In order to complete one rotation
in 24 hours, the earth spins 1,000
miles per hour! We don't feel the earth
moving as it rotates because the speed
is constant. If Earth suddenly stopped
moving, we would definitely feel it.

NOPE— THAT'S NOT IT, EITHER!

ROTATION is actually the cause of day and night. The earth rotates once every 24 hours. The side of the earth that faces the sun has day and the side that faces away from the sun has night. If rotation were the cause of the seasons, we'd have all four seasons in a single day!

So what IS the reason
for the seasons, you ask?

N Pole

OUR PLANET
IS TILTED!

Imagine a pole that passes
through the earth from north to
south—this is called Earth's axis.
Instead of being straight up and
down, it's tipped 23.5 degrees!

If Earth
wasn't tilted,
we would have
NO SEASONS
at all!

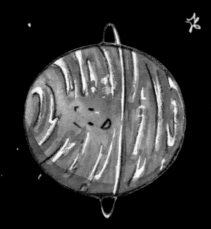

Scientists think Earth became tilted when a meteor the size
of Mars hit it, way back when our planet was first formed.
And it's not just us! Uranus is tilted sideways, and Venus is
tilted upside down, causing it to spin backward.

Earth's tilt affects how directly the light from the sun hits it. For instance, a spotlight puts out a very strong, hot light when it shines on you.

Presenting
A Midsummer
Night's Dream

The light also feels cooler.

Presenting
A Midsummer
Night's Dream

As you change the angle of the spotlight, the light appears dimmer.

This is because the same amount of light has to spread over a larger area.

Earth's tilt is also why shadows are different lengths throughout the seasons. They're shortest in summer because the sun is higher in the sky (just like that hot spotlight overhead).

The shadows grow a little longer in the fall.

Your shadow is longest in winter because the sun is so low.

Then, your shadow shortens again in the spring.

wondering what Earth's tilt looks like from space!
The Northern Hemisphere has summer when it is tilted toward the sun and the sun's light is most direct.

At the same time, the Southern Hemisphere has winter, when the sun's light is least direct.

When you look at Earth's orbit from the side, it looks like an oval. But from above, looking down on Earth's North Pole, the orbit appears more like a circle. However, many people mistakenly draw that view from above like an oval, showing the earth really close at one end and far away at the other.

This incorrect drawing has led many people to believe that summer occurs when the earth is closest to the sun instead of when the rays of light are most direct.

When the Southern Hemisphere is tilted toward the sun, it has summer and the Northern Hemisphere experiences winter.

June

September

December

March

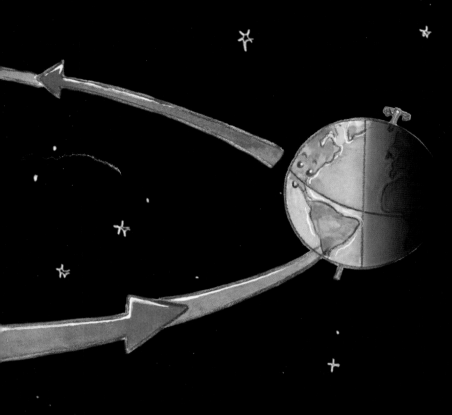

December

THIS!   NOT THIS!

Imagine a world where the sun never sets! The Arctic Circle is known as the "Land of the Midnight Sun" for this very reason. When the Northern Hemisphere has summer, the area near the North Pole is tilted so much toward the sun that on certain days, it never gets dark!

People who live in the Arctic Circle may go two or more months without seeing the sun set.

The opposite happens in winter. On certain days the Arctic Circle gets no light at all. It's in 24 hours of darkness!

and a **DRY** season.

The Incas, an ancient civilization that lived south of the equator, identified and based their calendar on two seasons: Planting and Harvest.

There are many ways to think of the seasons, but only one thing that causes them: the tilt of the earth.

Believing that Earth is closer to the sun in the summer is logical, it makes sense—but that doesn't make it right.

A good scientist always questions what she THINKS she knows.

How to Be a Scientist

The cause of the seasons might be the most common scientific misconception EVER! A misconception is a belief based on an incorrect understanding. Many kids, and even some adults, believe that the seasons are caused by the earth's distance from the sun.

How on Earth did people get such a wrong idea in the first place? About 400 years ago, an astronomer and mathematician named Johannes Kepler made an important discovery. People at that time understood that the earth and other planets revolve around the sun, but they weren't sure what their path looked like. Kepler realized that the earth's path around the sun is an ellipse, or oval, with the sun off-center.

It might have been better if Kepler said the path was *only slightly elliptical*. If you looked at Earth's orbit, you would see it's more like a circle than an oval. Unfortunately, he didn't, and since then many people have drawn diagrams of the earth and the sun that exaggerate that elliptical shape. As a result, many people falsely believe that there are huge differences between the distance of the earth and the sun at either end of the ellipse.

Now that YOU understand that the cause of the seasons is Earth's tilt, and not its distance from the sun, how can you demonstrate that to others?

Try This!

What you'll need:
- a flashlight
- a white piece of paper
- a pencil

STEP 1: Darken the room. Hold your flashlight about 6 inches above the white paper. Trace around the lit region that appears on the paper. Label this circle #1 and note its brightness.

STEP 2: Angle the flashlight slightly. Make sure it's still about 6 inches above the paper. Trace around this lit region and label it #2. Do you notice that the light looks dimmer and is taking up more space?

STEP 3: Continue this a few more times, angling the light more, but keeping it the same distance above the paper. As the flashlight angle increases, you'll see that the lit region continues getting larger and dimmer.

What's happening here? You're showing how indirect (more angled) rays of light give less energy or warmth than those that are direct. The flashlight always emits the same amount of light energy, but as you change its angle, that light covers more area on the paper. The same thing happens with the sun and the earth. The sun always emits the same amount of light energy, but because the earth is tilted, some areas receive direct light (overhead) and some receive indirect light (at an angle). As a result, the areas that receive direct light are warmer and those that have indirect light are colder.

Have fun experimenting and don't forget that the obvious answer isn't always the correct one! A good scientist always questions her assumptions.